ALL COOPED UP

Written and Illustrated by
Virginia Nevarez

◆ FriesenPress

Suite 300 - 990 Fort St
Victoria, BC, V8V 3K2
Canada

www.friesenpress.com

ISBN
978-1-5255-8753-5 (Hardcover)
978-1-5255-8752-8 (Paperback)
978-1-5255-8754-2 (eBook)

1. Juvenile Fiction, Social Issues, Emotions & Feelings

Distributed to the trade by The Ingram Book Company

Dedicated to

the Class of 2032, my kindergarteners at
Butte Vista School, my kindergarten team—
Robin, Vicki, Suzanne and Crystal—and
all those students who continue to dream
and shoot for the stars.

Just before the
first day of SPRING,
we all felt part of
this **uncertain thing.**

MAMA HEN said we
had to *come* INSIDE.
Didn't know we'd be in store
for an **unusual ride.**

2

So, my brothers and sisters
followed me up the **STOOP**
to our *humble* **LITTLE HOUSE,**
our **chicken coop.**

All of us *hopped,*
so **FREE** *and so* **LIGHT,**
up the **stoop** as the
SUN *settled down*
for the **night.**

6

Then *Mama* **HEN**
and *Papa* **ROOSTER**
came into the COOP.
Papa turned, *looked outside*
on the edge of the **stoop.**

"**Tomorrow, I'll crow
at sunrise, you know,
but we must stay inside
for a week or so.**"

8

Mama Hen *lifted* up her
soft, FEATHERED WING.
As all of us **huddled** under,
she began to *softly* SING.

"My dear little ones,
so sweet and so bright,
rest well, settle in,
you are safe on this night."

A **week** went by,
and we still *hunkered* **DOWN.**
In our **COOP,** on our STOOP,
no friends came around.

Then a week *slowly faded*
into a **MONTH,** maybe more.
But every day, **PAPA** *crowed*
like he'd always done before.

"Crow," sang Papa Rooster. **"Cock-a-doodle-doo."**
**"We're all in this together,
even you and you and you."**

Every morning, he *crowed* in
our own LITTLE PLACE,
in the back *near* the shack
in the **barnyard space.**

12

Then the **PIGS** all *oinked,*
and the **COWS** all *mooed.*
BEES *buzzed,* **LAMBS** *bleated,*
and the **DOVES** all *cooed.*

Then the **DOGS** sang, *"Woof,"*
and the **CAT** *meowed.*
We all used our voices and **sang out loud!**

14

It was a *barnyard* **CONCERT,**
though we all were *apart.*
We felt TOGETHER,
with each other in our **hearts.**

16

And although we **stayed** in
our own *little* HOME,
we were in this **TOGETHER**.
We were *not* alone.

18

"Crow," sang PAPA Rooster.
"Cock-a-doodle-doo."

20

"**Find** joy in all of
the *little* **THINGS** you do!
Try to **DANCE** and **SING,**

move around, and play.

Try to learn something **NEW**

each and **every day.**

And when the SUN goes down,

look around and say,

"Thank you, Family.

Today was a really good day."

Then we all *crawled* underneath
our MAMA'S WING
and *listened* to the SONG
that she liked to *sing*.

"My dear little ones,
so sweet and so bright,
rest well, settle in,
you are safe on this night."

ABOUT THE AUTHOR

All Cooped Up is Virginia Nevarez's first book, though she had been an artist all of her life. After studying at the Academy of Art University in San Francisco, she decided to become a teacher and bring her creativity to her students. She has been teaching for 30 years, 26 of those in kindergarten. She also has a master's degree in special education, with an emphasis in autism spectrum disorder.

When the school closures began in March 2020, due to the pandemic, Virginia, like other teachers around the world, had to figure out how to continue to teach her students from home and in ways that would be fun and interactive. Reflecting over this time and watching this shared experience unfold around the world, she started to draw and came up with *All Cooped Up*. This book is a gift to her kindergarten students and their families.

Virginia lives in Yuba City, California, with her husband, three wonderfully creative sons, and three playful cats.